SWIMMING WITH THE PLESIOSAUR

OTHER BOOKS IN THE SERIES:

ATTACK of the TYRANNOSAURUS

CHARGE of the TRICERATOPS

MARCH of the ANKYLOSAURUS

FLIGHT of the QUETZALCOATLUS

CATCHING the VELOCIRAPTOR

STAMPEDE of the EDMONTOSAURUS

SAVING the STEGOSAURUS

SWIMMING with the PLESIOSAUR

DINOSAUR COVE™

SWIMMING WITH THE PLESIOSAUR

BY
REX STONE

ILLUSTRATED BY
MIKE SPOOR

SCHOLASTIC INC.

New York   Toronto   London   Auckland
Sydney   Mexico City   New Delhi   Hong Kong

SPECIAL THANKS TO JAN BURCHETT
AND SARA VOGLER
TO MY GOOD FRIEND, ROMAN NOVOTNY – R.S.
TO CHRISTOPHER – M.S.

ISBN-13: 978-0-545-11246-8
ISBN-10: 0-545-11246-X

Dinosaur Cove series created by Working Partners Ltd., London.

Published by Scholastic Inc., 557 Broadway, New York, NY 10012, by arrangement with Working Partners Ltd. SCHOLASTIC, LITTLE APPLE, and associated logos are trademarks and/or registered trademarks of Scholastic Inc. DINOSAUR COVE is a registered trademark of Working Partners Ltd.

12 11 10 9   12 13 14/0

Printed in the U.S.A.
First printing, November 2009

FACT FILE

➡ JAMIE AND HIS BEST FRIEND, TOM, HAVE DISCOVERED A SECRET CAVE WITH FOSSILIZED DINOSAUR FOOTPRINTS AND, WHEN THEY PLACE THEIR FEET OVER EACH OF THE FOSSILS IN TURN, THEY ARE MAGICALLY TRANSPORTED TO A WORLD WITH REAL, LIVE DINOSAURS. THE JURASSIC PERIOD WAS KNOWN FOR HAVING LOTS OF SEA LIFE AND THE BOYS WANT TO SEE IT UP CLOSE. BUT NOT TOO CLOSE ...

JAMIE

- FULL NAME: JAMIE MORGAN
- AGE: 8 YEARS
- SIZE: 1 JATOM*
- TOP SPEED: 7 MPH
- LIKES: FOSSIL HUNTING AND LEARNING ABOUT DINOSAURS
- DISLIKES: BEING STUCK INDOORS

Jamie's eye

Jamie's foot

Jamie's hand

*NOTE: A JATOM IS THE SIZE OF JAMIE OR TOM: 4 FT TALL AND 60 LBS IN WEIGHT.

TOM

- FULL NAME: THOMAS CLAY
- AGE: 8 YEARS
- SIZE: 1 JATOM*
- TOP SPEED: 7 MPH
- LIKES: TRACKING ANIMALS AND EXPLORING WILDLIFE
- DISLIKES: RAINY DAYS

Tom's eye   Tom's hand

WANNA

- FULL NAME: WANNANOSAURUS
- AGE: 65 – 80 MILLION YEARS**
- SIZE: LESS THAN A JATOM*
- TOP SPEED: 30 MPH, ESPECIALLY WHEN BEING CHASED BY A T-REX
- LIKES: STINKY GINKGO FRUIT AND BANGING HIS HEAD ON TREE TRUNKS
- DISLIKES: SCARY DINOSAURS

Wanna's head   Wanna's foot

*NOTE: A JATOM IS THE SIZE OF JAMIE OR TOM: 4 FT TALL AND 60 LBS IN WEIGHT.
**NOTE: SCIENTISTS CALL THIS PERIOD THE LATE CRETACEOUS.

LIOPLEURODON

Liopleurodon's eye

Liopleurodon's teeth

Liopleurodon's fin

Liopleurodon's tail

- FULL NAME: LIOPLEURODON
- AGE: 155 – 160 MILLION YEARS**
- LENGTH: OVER 10 JATOMS*
- WEIGHT: OVER 370 JATOMS*
- LIKES: BEING THE FIERCEST AQUATIC PREDATOR OF ALL TIME; HUNTING TASTY ICHTHYOSAURS
- DISLIKES: WHEN FOOD GETS AWAY AND BEING CALLED A DINOSAUR. IT WAS A MARINE REPTILE.

*NOTE: A JATOM IS THE SIZE OF JAMIE OR TOM: 4 FT TALL AND 60 LBS IN WEIGHT.
**NOTE: SCIENTISTS CALL THIS PERIOD THE JURASSIC

DINOSAUR COVE

Village

Marina

Sealight Head

Hurry up, Tom! Jamie Morgan thought as a wave lapped around his ankles, swirling the sand beneath his bare feet.

Jamie was going snorkeling in Dinosaur Cove and his best friend, Tom Clay, was late. He scanned the empty beach, squinting in the sunshine.

Suddenly, he spotted Tom running across the sand with his snorkel and mask dangling over one arm, a bodyboard in the other, and his binoculars around his neck.

"You can't go bodyboarding today," Jamie called. "The sea's as flat as a Frisbee."

"I'm not going bodyboarding." Tom grinned, skidding to a halt. "In fact I'm not going in *that* sea at all."

"Not even snorkeling?" asked Jamie, disappointed.

Tom shook his head. "Not here."

"Near the headland then?" asked Jamie. Tom had lived in Dinosaur Cove all his life, so he knew the best places.

"No, much farther away than that." Tom's grin was nearly splitting his face. "But we can be there in an instant."

"You mean . . ." Jamie began.

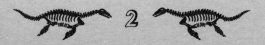

"The Jurassic ocean!" Tom finished.

Jamie and Tom shared a fantastic secret. They'd found a way to visit a world of living dinosaurs.

"Cool!" exclaimed Jamie. He could already feel bubbles of excitement inside. "Good thing I never go anywhere without my backpack."

"You've still got the Jurassic ammonite?" Tom asked as the boys raced toward the cliff path on Smugglers' Point. On their last visit, the boys had discovered that the ammonite fossil they carried with them determined which time period they visited.

"I've got it," Jamie replied. "But why do you have a bodyboard when we're going snorkeling?"

"It's for Wanna," Tom explained as they neared the rocks that led up to their secret cave. "He can ride while we swim. It's even got one of his prehistoric friends on it." He stopped at the top of the cliff and turned the board over. A fearsome-looking reptile with four powerful flippers had its mouth open to show off sharp, scary-looking teeth.

Jamie took his Fossil Finder out of his backpack and keyed in *SEA MONSTERS. LEE-OH-PLUR-AH-DON*, he read. *MOST SUCCESSFUL AQUATIC HUNTER IN THE JURASSIC, THE LIOPLEURODON IS A TYPE OF PLESIOSAUR*. Jamie stuffed the Fossil Finder back into his backpack. "Looks like a plesiosaur wouldn't call Wanna his friend. It would call him dinner."

The boys scrambled up the rocks to the old Smugglers' Cave and the hidden entrance to Dino World. They squeezed into the secret chamber at the back, and Jamie shone his flashlight onto the line of fossilized footprints.

"Ready for action?" said Jamie.

"You bet!" Tom replied.

They put their feet into each clover-shape print. "One,

two,

three,

four . . .

five!"

In an instant, Jamie and Tom were walking out among the huge trees of the Jurassic jungle. Giant dragonflies buzzed around them like model airplanes in the steaming air.

"Phew! It's as hot as ever," said Tom, wiping his forehead. "Just right for a swim."

Grunk!

There was a rustling in the spiky horsetail plants nearby, and a little green-and-brown wannanosaurus burst out.

"Hello, Wanna!" Tom patted their dinosaur friend on his hard domed head, and Wanna wagged his tail in excitement.

Jamie picked some ginkgoes from an overhanging tree. "Good thing his favorite fruit grows in Cretaceous *and* Jurassic times." He tossed two to Wanna and hid the rest in his backpack. Wanna gobbled up the smelly snacks and rushed around on his stumpy legs, giving the boys sticky licks.

Jamie took out his notebook with the new map of the Jurassic Dino World. "This says that the sea is southwest from the cave. Got your compass?"

"'Course." Tom pulled it out and pointed to the southwest. "Through the trees here."

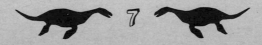

The three friends set off over the hills,
walking through the trees and deep ferns until
they arrived on the edge of a cliff, looking out
over the beautiful ocean. To their right was a
calm, sparkling bay shielded from the waves
by a line of jet-black rocks poking up out of
the water.

"Awesome!" exclaimed Tom. "With those rocks as barriers, that bay's just like a swimming pool."

"The perfect place for snorkeling," said Jamie. "And we can climb down that path where the cliff's crumbled away."

"Last one to the beach is a sea slug!" yelled Tom.

CHAPTER 2

"**B**eat you!" Jamie laughed as he clambered over the last of the slippery black slate rocks onto the sand.

"Only just," said Tom, sliding down beside him. "Anyway, Wanna's the sea slug."

Wanna scampered happily up behind.

"Do you think he remembers our last trip to the seaside?" asked Jamie. "He had quite an adventure with his flying reptile friends."

Tom grinned. "Who knows what goes on inside that domed head?"

As the boys headed along the sand, Tom pointed to the biggest rock out in the bay. "That rock looks like the back of a sea monster with a fin sticking up in the middle."

"We'll call it Fin Rock," Jamie decided. The tall rock stood like a gate to the open sea, and waves splashed up against it on the ocean side. Beyond the line of rocks, Jamie could see something leaping out of the ocean. "Wow!"

Tom saw it, too, and looked through his binoculars. "There's more than one!" He thrust the binoculars at Jamie.

Jamie knew what they were right away.

"They're ichthyosauruses."
He flipped open his Fossil
Finder and punched the
keys. The image of a
pointy-nosed prehistoric
dolphin flashed up.
ICK-THEE-OH-SOR, he read.
*ATE FISH AND SQUID. EXTINCT
BY THE CRETACEOUS AGE.*

"They look like they're having fun," Tom
said. "We should, too. Let's go snorkeling!"

They dumped the backpack, Tom's binoculars,
and their T-shirts and shoes on a dry rock,
grabbed their masks and snorkels, and waded
into the warm, shallow water. Tom carried the
bodyboard.

The water was so clear that Jamie could see
his toes and the pebbles on the sand.

Wanna dashed after them, but skidded to a
halt at the sight of the tiny waves.

"You scaredy-cat!" Tom laughed. "They won't hurt you."

"I know what'll get him in." Jamie ran back onto the beach to his backpack and pulled out a ginkgo fruit.

He backed slowly into the water, keeping it just out of Wanna's reach. The little dinosaur followed eagerly, but when the water lapped over his feet, he darted away again.

Jamie pretended to take a big bite out of the stinky ginkgo. "Yum, yum!"

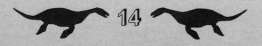

Wanna licked his lips
and took a few steps forward,
wading up to his knees in
the water.

"That's it, boy," Jamie
said. "Come and get
your tasty snack." He
put the ginkgo on the
bodyboard as Tom
held it still.

Grunk!

Wanna scrambled
onto the bodyboard,
making it wobble in
the water. Jamie held
Wanna's waist as the
little dinosaur got his
balance.

"He looks like a
surfer," chuckled Tom,
letting go of the board.

grunk!

grunk!

grunk!

"Champion of the waves," said Jamie.

But when Wanna bent down to eat his ginkgo, he overbalanced and somersaulted into the sea. He sat in the shallow water looking very surprised.

"Poor old Wanna," said Jamie, trying not to laugh. The boys helped him on again. This time Wanna managed to stay afloat, but looked mournfully at the ginkgo, which

was floating
away. Jamie
grabbed it and Wanna
ate it gratefully.

"I reckon you've
earned that," said Tom.

Jamie put his hand
firmly through the
loop of the bodyboard's
rope. "Stay still and I'll pull
you along," he said to Wanna.

"Masks on!" declared Tom.
The boys pulled their
masks over their faces.

"Check!" said Jamie.

"Snorkels in."

Tom placed the snorkel in his mouth and gave an excited thumbs-up.

The boys waded out until the water came up to their armpits and then started swimming, putting their faces in the water so that their snorkels pointed up into the air. Jamie looked down, breathing through his snorkel. Below him, small plants waved in the gentle current and weird, colorful sea creatures darted up and down. An electric-blue sea slug crept over a rock. Then a group of squid-like creatures came swimming by. Their spiral shells were wonderful colors: blues, greens, and purples.

Real live ammonites! Jamie thought. *They're so bright.* The ammonites were nothing like

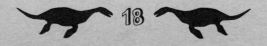

18

the brown and gray fossils he and Tom often dug up back at Dinosaur Cove.

He could see Tom was having fun, too. He made an O shape with his thumb and forefinger, the OK sign for divers. Tom signed back and made a face like a blubbery fish. Jamie burst out laughing, and they both came up, gasping for air.

Wanna grunked cheerfully at them. He was obviously enjoying himself as much as they were.

The boys looked down again. A shoal of large cuttlefish drifted past.

They seemed to change color as they swam, from yellow to orange to blue. Jamie watched, fascinated, as their eight arms and two long tentacles explored the sand below them.

Tom dived below the water, pretending to film them as if he were making a documentary, until they disappeared into some fronds of sea kelp. But Tom wasn't paying attention to where he was swimming, and one of his legs became tangled in the underwater leaves.

As quick as he could, Jamie dived down into the tangle to pull his friend free.

"Thanks, Jamie," Tom said as they surfaced.

"That would have made a good TV show," Jamie joked, adjusting his mask on his face. "Attack of the Killer Kelp!"

Tom laughed, but stopped suddenly.
"Wait — where's the bodyboard?"

Jamie glanced down at his wrist. The rope was gone! "It must have slipped off." The boys looked around frantically for their little dino friend.

"Over there," said Tom, pointing.

Wanna was sitting happily on his board, peering down into the water, completely unaware that he was drifting toward the deep, dangerous ocean beyond Fin Rock.

"Wanna!" yelled Jamie in alarm.

The boys swam quickly through the water after their friend, breathing through their snorkels so that they could swim as fast as possible. Jamie could see the seabed sloping away beneath him and the water getting deeper and deeper.

He pulled hard with his arms and kicked furiously. Glancing up through his splashes, he could see that they were nearing the wide gap in the rock barrier and the rough, foaming water beyond. Wanna was going to be swept out to sea! Jamie couldn't let that happen.

Suddenly, Jamie was close enough to see the bright yellow rope ahead of him. He tried to grab it but it slipped through his fingers. Wanna and the bodyboard had reached the gap next to Fin Rock and were bobbing on the choppy water at the edge of the shallow bay. Beyond was the ocean, so deep and dark that Jamie couldn't see the bottom.

He kicked forward again and grabbed the loop of the rope, holding on with all his strength as the board tugged against him in the rough water.

"Got him!" he yelled to Tom, his snorkel banging against his cheek.

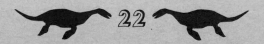

"Just in time," Tom said as he swam up. "Let's get away from here."

Jamie could feel the board wobbling violently in the waves. Wanna gave a frightened grunk.

"Don't worry, boy," Jamie told him. "You'll soon be safe."

But the little dinosaur didn't seem to understand. He kicked his feet and waved his tail wildly, eyes wide with fear.

"No, Wanna!" shouted Tom. "Stop!"

The board rocked more and more violently until . . .

SPLASH!
Wanna disappeared under the water.

CHAPTER 3

Jamie dropped the rope, took a deep breath, and dived. He caught hold of Wanna's flailing front leg and kicked for the surface. Wanna emerged, spluttering, then went under again. Jamie had taken lifeguard classes, but they hadn't gone over how to save a dinosaur from drowning! He swam around behind Wanna, avoiding the flapping feet, and grasped him around his neck, pulling him to the surface. Jamie had to kick hard to stay afloat as Wanna struggled in panic.

"Keep still, boy!" he spluttered as he swam to the edge of Fin Rock. When Jamie finally reached the rock, Tom helped give Wanna a shove to get the little dinosaur up onto the flat part of Fin Rock. Jamie stayed in the water, clinging to the rock, to get his breath back.

Safely on the rock, Wanna sneezed and then spotted some seaweed.

Grunk!

He started eating the slimy leaves as if nothing had happened. Jamie smiled and hauled himself out. He pulled his mask down around his neck, like Tom had done.

"Looks like we've lost the bodyboard," Tom said, pointing out to sea where the board floated away with the waves. "And if scientists discover a bodyboard next to a dinosaur fossil, we could mess up all of history. Not to mention that we're going to have a hard time getting Wanna back to the beach."

Jamie groaned. "I'm sorry. It's all my fault. I dropped the rope."

"You were saving me from killer kelp at the time." Tom grinned. "Anyway, it was my stupid idea to bring Wanna snorkeling."

Jamie watched the bodyboard being tossed by the rough sea as he tried to think of how to get Wanna back to shore, when suddenly, a sleek, blue-gray creature jumped over the board, diving smoothly back beneath the surface.

"An ichthyosaurus," breathed Tom. "Awesome!"

"It's two ickies," Jamie said as another ichthyosaurus batted the bodyboard with its nose, flicking it up into the air like a sea lion with a beach ball.

"Three!" yelled Tom in excitement as one more head popped up in the choppy sea. It caught the board between its teeth and swam away, its friends following behind.

"They're playing with it!" Jamie said.

"I think they're bringing it back," said Tom.

The ichthyosauruses swam right up to Fin Rock. One of them nudged the bodyboard toward the boys.

28

CLICK, CLICK!

Tom and Jamie bent down to get a close look at the sleek marine reptile eyeing them from the water.

"It's smaller than the other two," said Jamie. "I reckon it's a young one, but it's still as big as a dolphin."

"It has a dolphin's snout," agreed Tom. "Only longer and thinner. And an extra set of flippers."

"And plenty of teeth," Jamie replied. "But it seems friendly. Look at that silly grin on its face. And those huge eyes."

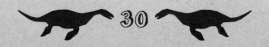

click!

click!

CLICK, CLICK, CLICK!

The icky gave the bodyboard another nudge so that it banged against the rock.

"Thanks!" Tom laughed. "We'll be more careful next time." He fished the board out of the water.

Grunk! Wanna agreed.

The icky waved its flippers and chirped loudly, diving forward in a perfect arc and speeding into the shallow water of the bay. Its friends plunged after it.

"I think they're playing tag," Jamie said.

Tom slid the bodyboard down to the calm water on the bay side of the rock.

"Better get Wanna back to dry land."

Jamie put his mask on, his snorkel back in, and then jumped into the sea. "Come on, boy," he coaxed, patting the board.

Grunk! Wanna sounded anxious.

He began to stamp his feet.

"You'll be all right, I promise," said Tom. "We'll keep the board steady."

Grunk, grunk, grunk!

Wanna was jumping up and down now, drumming his tail on the rock. His eyes were fixed on the ocean.

"What's wrong?" asked Jamie.

"He's frightened," said Tom. "And so are the ickies." In the bay, the ichthyosauruses were now circling anxiously, making an urgent, clamoring whistle.

Jamie pulled his mask on and ducked under the surface.

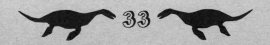

From the depths of the ocean, a huge, dark shape was swimming up through the water, heading for the bay. It had a long, crocodile-like head and four strong flippers on its massive body. It was the real-life monster on the bodyboard — a plesiosaur, the deadliest creature in the ocean.

And it was coming straight for him!

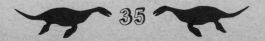

CHAPTER 4

"**P**lesiosaur," spluttered Jamie. "Got to get out!"

Tom didn't waste a second. He hauled his friend onto the rock and pulled the board up after him.

"Thanks," panted Jamie, pulling down his mask. "That sea monster's huge."

They turned to see the plessy break the surface of the water. It was at least five times as long as one of the ickies. Its massive jaws stretched like a grin, showing razor-sharp teeth that glistened in the sun.

The boys watched in horror as the plessy swam straight past Fin Rock and into the bay.

"It's after the ickies," said Tom.

The ickies waited in the bay, watching the plessy approach. Suddenly, with a flick of their tails, they shot toward the gap in the rocks, trying to escape into the deep ocean. But the plessy was too big for the ickies to get around.

"They're trapped!" said Jamie.

The plessy kept its enormous body blocking their escape route to the ocean, and each time the ickies tried to make for the open sea, the monster snapped with its fearsome teeth. The water churned like a whirlpool as the creatures struggled.

"The little one's getting tired," said Tom.

"And that nasty plessy knows it," added Jamie grimly.

The little icky made another dash for it, but the sea monster plunged down under the water with a huge splash. Jamie and Tom held their breath. When the plessy's head rose again they could see the young ichthyosaurus thrashing helplessly in its jaws. Its friends called to it anxiously.

"Oh, no!" Jamie felt horrible watching the frantic icky.

The plessy shook its prize in triumph. But one of the ickies dived and swam at the monster, head butting it hard on the soft underside of its belly. As it turned on its attacker, the second icky rammed it from the other side, making the plessy let go of its prey, which darted off to its friends.

"One–nil to the ickies!" yelled Tom, almost falling off the rock in delight.

"They haven't won yet," Jamie reminded him. "They're still trapped."

"They helped us," said Tom determinedly. "We have to help them."

"You're right," agreed Jamie. "But how?"

Tom quickly scanned their craggy island and went over to a spur of rock with a deep crack in it. He slid his fingers in and heaved.

"This is no time for weightlifting," said Jamie.

"I'm not weightlifting," puffed Tom, red in the face with the effort. "This rock is loose. We can . . . throw it . . . at the plessy. Might scare it off."

Jamie helped. Soon the rock came away. The boys picked it up between them and staggered to the water's edge.

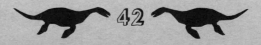

"We'll give that creature something to think about!" shouted Tom. "One, *two*, *three*, HEAVE!"

They lobbed the rock as hard as they could. It fell with a great splash near the monster. But the plessy didn't flinch.

It plowed on through the water after its prey. Its thick tail slapped down, splashing a huge wave over Fin Rock. The boys clung on to the fin-shape rock, digging fingers and toes into any hold they could find. Wanna clung to the boys and grunked anxiously.

"That was close," gasped Tom.

"Quick!" yelled Jamie. "The bodyboard."

The board was floating away into the bay. Tom grabbed the bodyboard's rope just in time.

"Good save," said Jamie.

Tom was just putting the loop around his wrist to make it secure when Jamie noticed that they were in trouble. "Uh-oh!" Jamie shouted. "The monster's seen it."

"Wait," Tom said. "I've got an idea."

Jamie saw the plessy's beady eyes above the surface of the water. They were fixed on the bobbing board. "That monster will break it to pieces," Jamie said.

"Hang on," Tom replied. He gave the rope a shake, making the bodyboard shudder. The plessy glided toward it like a deadly crocodile after its prey, its jaws opening wide. Suddenly it lunged, but Tom quickly flicked the board up and onto the rock and the plessy missed entirely.

"It's just like trout fishing," he shouted. "Though I hope I don't catch that monster!"

Jamie gave a whoop of delight. "Go, Tom!" he called. "The plessy's forgotten all about the ickies."

Tom threw the board out. Again the plessy lunged and Tom jerked it away.

Jamie looked at the ickies' progress and saw that they had made it to the gap in the rocks. "The ickies are escaping!" Jamie cried, but then Tom slipped on the wet rock. He couldn't throw the board out again.

"You do it!" Tom said, throwing the rope up to Jamie.

Jamie grabbed the rope, knowing he needed to keep the monster busy until the ichthyosauruses were safely away. He flung the bodyboard out like Tom had done — but this time the plessy was ready. As soon as it saw the bright board slapping down onto the water, it grabbed it in its teeth and pulled hard. Jamie didn't have a chance to let go of the rope.

He was catapulted off the rock and into the water!

splash!

CHAPTER 5

The water roared in Jamie's ears as he was dragged along the surface by the sea monster into the bay. White foam swirled around him, and he wished he had had his mask on. Everything was blurry, but he could still see through the water. Suddenly the pulling stopped. Jamie looked ahead and could just make out through the water that the plesiosaur had turned. It floated on the water, its beady eyes right above the surface. They were looking straight at him.

It let go of the bodyboard.

Oh, no, thought Jamie. *I'm dinner!*

As the huge gray body slipped under the surface of the water, coming toward him, Jamie swam frantically for the rock.

He could just hear Tom shouting, "Hurry, Jamie!"

Jamie knew he couldn't outswim the plessy, but then he remembered something Tom had told him about predators losing interest when their prey stopped moving. He had nothing to lose. Jamie took a huge

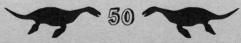

breath and stopped swimming. He quickly made a star with his arms and legs and lay there, floating facedown in the water.

He watched, his heart pounding hard, as the plessy swam in a circle below, watching him.

Jamie knew he couldn't move a muscle. The bodyboard rope was still tied around his wrist, tugging at him. He had to fight to keep his arm still, but his plan was working!

The sea monster wasn't attacking anymore. It had lost interest. But Jamie knew that as soon as he lifted his head for air it could be back on to him like a shot.

Please go! he thought, desperately willing the sea monster to swim away. But it didn't. Jamie felt as if his lungs were going to burst.

Suddenly he heard a great barrage of squeaking, clicking, and whistling in the water.

Something was coming from the deep ocean. The plessy had heard it, too.

It whipped around to see what it was. Jamie took his chance. He lifted his head and gulped in air.

Then he saw a wonderful sight. A large pod of sleek gray ichthyosauruses was speeding toward the bay. They leaped over the waves, calling to one another — and Jamie could see their three little icky friends leading the charge!

They made straight for the plessy and began to ram it from all sides. It thrashed around, trying to ward off the furious attack.

Jamie swam for the rock and, with Tom's help, scrambled out of the water. Wanna grabbed the bodyboard in his teeth and pulled it onto the rock.

"Go, ickies!" yelled Tom. "You can beat that monster."

The plessy reared and plunged, thrashing out angrily to shake off the whirling mass of ickies. But there were too many. They battered and rammed from all sides.

The boys and Wanna watched as the beast swished its massive tail, sending a final huge wave breaking over Fin Rock, then fled for the open sea.

Jamie and Tom leaped up and down in delight while Wanna grunted eagerly. The sea monster had been beaten!

CHAPTER 6

"That was awesome!" breathed Jamie.

"Those ickies saved your life." Tom grinned.

Jamie nodded. "Too right! They fought off the fiercest creature in the Jurassic ocean!"

"And they look really pleased about it," said Tom, pointing.

The pod of ickies was swimming all around Fin Rock, their sleek bodies arcing in and out of the waves. Wanna grunted happily at them.

"Thank you!" Jamie shouted. "You were great." He turned to Tom. "Shame we don't know icky language."

"Looks like they understood anyway," replied Tom. The ickies were sending back a chorus of clicks and whistles. "I think they're saying, 'You're welcome.'"

"Let's get back to dry land," said Jamie, putting his mask back on. "Hop on board, Wanna. The water's safe now."

Grunk! Wanna looked at the bodyboard, which was punctured with large plessy teeth holes.

"Don't worry, boy," Tom assured him. "It's still seaworthy."

Jamie slid into the water, pulling the bodyboard behind him. Tom held it steady and Wanna wobbled on board. Holding one side each, the boys kicked off for shore.

"I can hear something behind us," Tom shouted suddenly.

Jamie spun around, spluttering as his mouth filled with water. Then he burst out laughing. "We've got an escort."

It was the three young ickies swimming along behind the boys, clicking and whistling.

Soon Jamie and Tom were close enough to the shore to stand in the waist-deep water.

The smallest icky swam around their legs, gently butting them as if to say good-bye. Then it sped off to its friends and the three of them swam swiftly away, heading for the open sea.

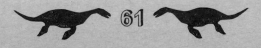

"Thanks again," called Jamie after them, pulling off his mask entirely.

Grunk!

Wanna jumped off the bodyboard and splashed the last few steps to the beach.

The boys picked up their things and made their way back to the cave. Jamie pointed to the huge teeth marks in Tom's board. "How are we going to explain this?"

"We could say it got attacked by a shark," suggested Tom.

"No one will believe that," Jamie replied.

"Well, they won't believe what really happened to it."

Wanna stuck out his tongue and gave the bodyboard a lick. Then he trotted off toward the cave. When they got close, Wanna began to gather leaves and twigs in his teeth.

"He's making
himself a nest,"
said Tom.

"Let's help," said
Jamie, grabbing a handful
of ferns. The boys got to work,
gathering sticks and ferns.

Wanna laid a few twigs down, then nudged
them here and there, but when Jamie went to
put some branches into the structure, Wanna
grunked loudly.

"I think he's saying they're the wrong way up."
Tom laughed.

Jamie flipped the branches over. "Is that
better?"

Grunk, grunk!

Wanna wagged his tail. Soon he was curled
up in his Jurassic nest.

"Sleep tight, boy," said Tom. The boys had
seen on their last visit that Wanna knew how

to go back to the Cretaceous any time he
wanted, so they said good-bye to their faithful
friend and stepped backward in the footprints.

As the boys emerged into the bright sunlight
of Dinosaur Cove, they were surprised to see
a crowd of people gathered on the shoreline
below.

"What's going on?" Tom asked.

"There's Grandpa," said Jamie. "Let's find out."

They scrambled down to the beach as fast as
they could.

Everyone was staring and pointing out to
sea. Tom made sure he kept the bodyboard
behind him so no one would notice the
teeth marks.

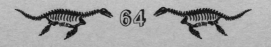

"I was wondering where you two had gone," Grandpa called when he spotted them. "You've been missing all the fun."

He nodded out toward the bay. As the boys watched, the enormous body of a sleek gray creature broke the surface of the sea. A tall spout of water shot into the air. A moment later, a gigantic whale leaped out of the waves. The crowd clapped and cheered.

"Don't see many whales in these parts." Jamie's grandfather beamed.

"Looks like Dinosaur Cove has got its own sea monster," Jamie whispered to Tom with a wink.

"But not as scary as the one back in Dino World," Tom whispered back.

"I definitely prefer this one," Jamie said.

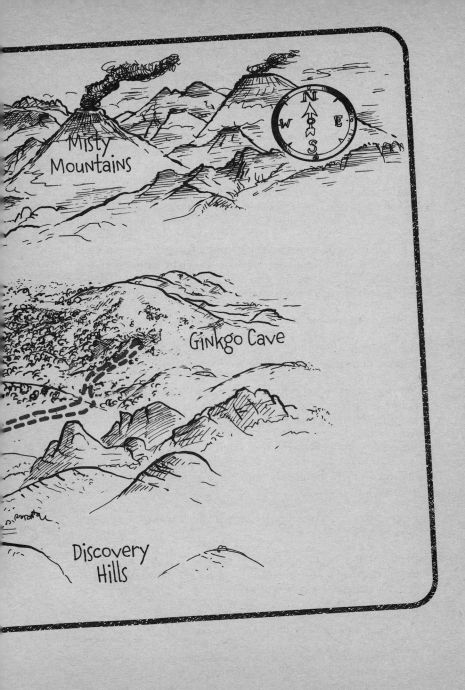

GLOSSARY

Ammonite — an extinct animal with octopus-like legs, and often a spiral-shape shell, that lived in the ocean.

Cretaceous — from about 65 to 150 million years ago, this time period was home to the widest variety of dinosaur and insect life of any period. Birds replaced winged dinosaurs, while in the sea, sharks and rays multiplied.

Cuttlefish — a marine mollusk — not a fish, similar to a squid or octopus, with large W-shaped eyes, eight arms, and two tentacles. When they are threatened, they squirt an ink-like fluid or change color to blend in with their surroundings.

Ginkgo — a tree native to China called a "living fossil" because fossils of it have been found dating back millions of years, yet they are still around today. Also known as the stink-bomb tree because of its smelly apricot-like fruit.

Ichthyosaurus — an extinct marine reptile that looked like a dolphin but had long jaws with sharp teeth, a fin on its back, four flippers, and a tail.

Jurassic — from about 150 to 200 million years ago, the Jurassic age was warm and humid, with lush jungle cover and great marine diversity. Large dinosaurs ruled on land, while the first birds took to the air.

Kelp — large brown seaweed. Offers shelter for some sea life and food for others.

Liopleurodon — one of the biggest and scariest meat-eating marine reptiles in the Jurassic sea, with four powerful flippers, and a large head, but a short neck.

Plesiosaur — a class of large meat-eating sea reptiles with a broad body, large flippers, and a short tail. The name means "near lizard."

Wannanosaurus — a dinosaur that only ate plants and used its hard, flat skull to defend itself. Named after the place it was discovered: Wannano, in China.

WATCH OUT!
I'M COMING SOON . . .

Read all of Tom and Jamie's dinosaur adventures!